SLEEP RHYMES AROUND THE WORLD

EDITED BY JANE YOLEN

ILLUSTRATED BY 17 INTERNATIONAL ARTISTS

Wordsong / Boyds Mills Press

For Kent and Jody and their big Honesdale family

Published by Wordsong

Boyds Mills Press, Inc.

A Highlights Company

815 Church Street

Honesdale, Pennsylvania 18431

Printed in China

Publisher Cataloging-in-Publication Data

Yolen, Jane.

Sleep rhymes around the world / edited by Jane Yolen ;

illustrated by 17 international artists.—1st ed.

[40]p. : col. ill. ; cm.

Summary: A collection of lullabies from seventeen different countries,

each illustrated by an artist native to the country.

ISBN 1-56397-923-3

1. Children's poetry. 2. Lullabies. [1. Bedtime—Poetry.

2. Poetry—Collections.] I. Title.

808.81—dc20   1994   CIP

Library of Congress Catalog Card Number 93-60244

First Boyds Mills Press paperback edition, 2000

Book designed by Joy Chu

The text of this book is set in Tiffany Roman and Italic.

10 9 8 7 6 5 4 3 2 1

Table of Contents

. . .

About the author and illustrators   *40*

Introduction

· · ·

Although I don't remember my mother singing lullabies to me, I know she did. My father did, too, accompanying himself with his funny little ukulele. They told me all about it when I was raising my own children.

Mothers and fathers all over the world sing and tell lullaby rhymes to their sleepy children, whether those children doze in tents or huts or apartment houses that reach to the sky.

When I started to collect rhymes for this book—from books and from friends who had been brought up in countries all over the world—it was with a sense of recognition that I came to the poems. For even if I had never heard them before, they were familiar.

Here are just a few of those lullabies set down for you, along with illustrations drawn by artists from the countries where those songs originate.

Not all languages are written in Roman alphabet letters. Some languages—such as Korean—have their own alphabets. For languages such as these, we have created phonetic translations, or transliterations, of the words so you can "hear" how these rhymes sound.

—*Jane Yolen*

THAILAND

Chao non bai

Yen pra-pai ma ruay-ruay

Mae cha pa pai non duay

Cha klom hai chao non

Mue-sai cha pad wee

Mue-kwa nee pen Chamorn

Sao-noy chao ya on

Chao puan-non kong mue — euy

Take an afternoon nap, my baby.

When the cool, constant breeze caresses you

I'll cuddle you to sleep, very near to me.

I'll lull you to sleep with my songs.

With my left hand as a fan I'll cool you,

With my right hand as a whisk I'll protect you.

Don't cry, my baby,

Dear sleeping friend of mine.

Non sia terd

Kwan chao kerd nai kaw-Bua

Lieng wai . . .

Wang cha dai pen puan-tua

Toon-hua chao kon-diew — euy

Sleep, my baby, sleep.

You were born among the lotus;

I picked you up and brought you up.

Hope you'll be my lifetime friend, dear,

Oh, my one and only dearest friend.

With thanks to Somboon Singkamanan and Pensri Tongyai

ITALY

Er a la vò.
Che beddu stu nomu.
Cu ci lu misi e un glantumu.
Bo, bo, bo, bo.
Durmi nicu e fa la vò.

Sleep until dawn.
How beautiful your name is.
He who gave it to you is a fine fellow.
Bo, bo, bo, bo.
Sleep, little one, go to sleep.

Er a la vò.
Sunnuzzu veni.
Veni a cavaddu e veniri a peri.
Bo, bo, bo, bo.
Durmi nicu e fa la vò.

Sleep until dawn.
Let sleep come.
Come on horseback, and do not come on foot.
Bo, bo, bo, bo.
Sleep, little one, go to sleep.

Nonna, nonnarella,
O lupe s'ha magnate la pecurella.
E pecurella mie commu faciste
Quanne mbocca lu lupe te vediste?
Nonna giú, nonna su, nonna giú,
Il bambino di Gesú!
Di Gesú di la Madonna,
Di Papà quando ritorna.
Papà é ritornate,
Il bambino si é dormentate!
Nonna giú, nonna su.

Sleep, sleep, dear heart,
The wolf has eaten the lamb.
And lamb, what did you do
When you found yourself in the wolf's mouth?
Sleepy-down, sleepy-up, sleepy-down,
The child of Jesus!
Of Jesus of the Virgin Mary,
And of Papa when he comes home.
Papa, he is returning,
And the baby has fallen asleep!
Sleepy-down, sleepy-up.

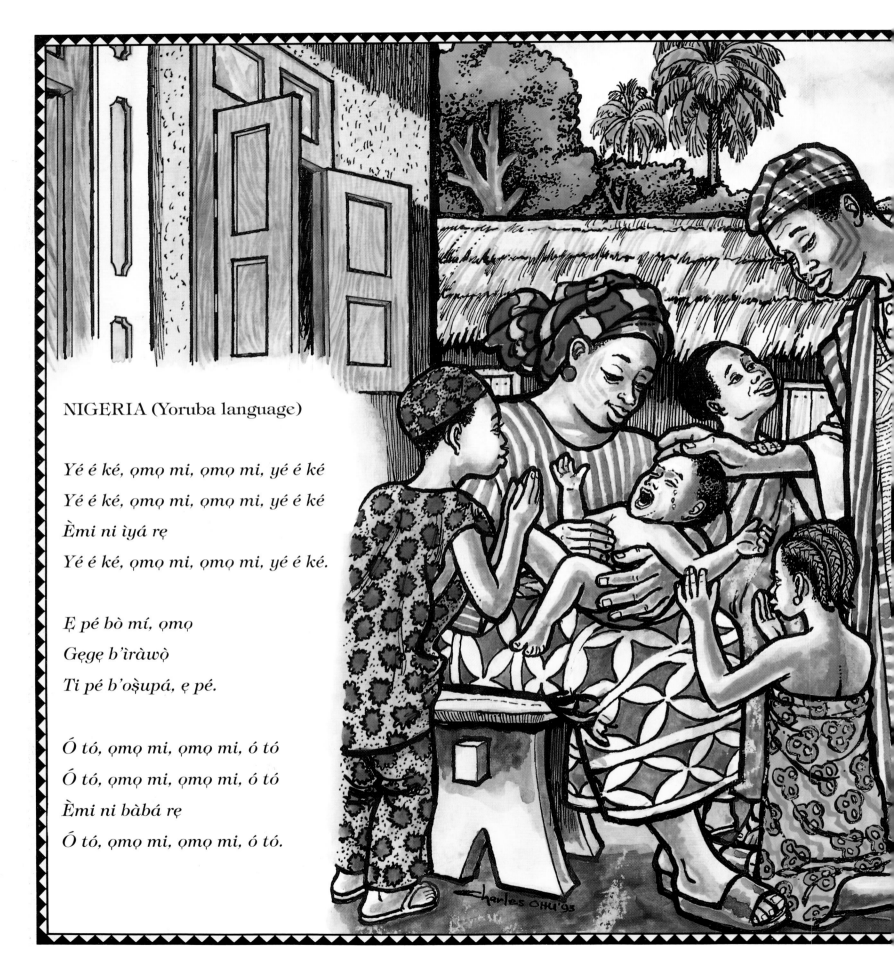

NIGERIA (Yoruba language)

Yé é ké, ọmọ mi, ọmọ mi, yé é ké
Yé é ké, ọmọ mi, ọmọ mi, yé é ké
Èmi ni ìyá rẹ
Yé é ké, ọmọ mi, ọmọ mi, yé é ké.

Ẹ pé bò mí, ọmọ
Gẹgẹ b'ìràwọ̀
Ti pé b'oṣupá, ẹ pé.

Ó tó, ọmọ mi, ọmọ mi, ó tó
Ó tó, ọmọ mi, ọmọ mi, ó tó
Èmi ni bàbá rẹ
Ó tó, ọmọ mi, ọmọ mi, ó tó.

Do not cry, my child,
O do not cry, my little one,
For I, your mother, am here.
O do not cry, my child.

Gather round me, children,
Gather round me
Like stars round the moon,
Gather round me.

Hush-a-bye, my child,
O hush-a-bye, my little one,
For I, your father, am here.
O hush-a-bye, my child.

WALES

Holl amranthir sêr ddywedant,
Ar hyd y nos.
Dyma'r ffordd i fro gogoniant,
Ar hyd y nos.
Golau arall yw'r tywyllwch,
I arddangos gwir bryderthwch,
Teulu'r nefoedd mewn tawelwch,
Ar hyd y nos.

O mor siriol gwenna'r seren,
Ar hyd y nos.
I oleud chwaer ddiaren,
Ar hyd y nos.
Nos yw henaint pan ddaw cystudd,
Ond i harddu dyn ai hwyrddydd,
Rhown ein golau gwan in gilydd,
Ar hyd y nos.

Sleep, my love, and peace attend thee,
All through the night;
Guardian angels God will lend thee,
All through the night.
Soft the drowsy hours are creeping,
Hill and vale in slumber steeping,
I my loving vigil keeping,
All through the night.

Angels watching ever round thee,
All through the night;
In thy slumbers close surround thee,
All through the night.
They should of all fears disarm thee,
No forebodings should alarm thee,
They will let no peril harm thee,
All through the night.

Kotyku, kotyku,
Deh ty buvav,
Shcho ty chuvav?

Ya pid vikonechkom
kho drimav...
Mur-mur, mur-mur, mur-mur.

Kitty cat, kitty cat,
Where have you been,
What have you seen?

I have been quietly dreaming
under the window...
Purr-purr, purr-purr, purr-purr.

SLOVENIA

Z neba padajo kapljice,
zaspančkan zapri svoje očice.
Aja-tu-t-aja-zaspančkan si-ti,
ker nebo poje in joče,
zaspančkati te hoče.
Aja-tu-t-aja-zaspančkan si-ti,
ker nebo poje in joče,
zaspančkati te hoče.

Raindrops are falling from the skies,
tired, sleepy, close your eyes.
Tired and sleepy,
while the skies are weeping,
weeping and singing you their lullabies.
Tired and sleepy,
while the skies are weeping,
weeping and singing you their lullabies.

Mirno spavaj, dete zlato,
Bog naj te zaziblje v raj.
Z angelci na božjo trato
pojdi se igrat sedaj.

V tebi sreče sonce sije,
v tebi klije sto lepot,
milost božja nate lije,
varje angela perot.

Dokler v sebi boš hranilo
čistost teh otroških dni,
vedno se boš napotilo
v raj, kjer Bog živi.

Baby darling, sleep now gently,
God will rock you lovingly.
And with angels in His gardens
you will play so blissfully.

Happiness from you is shining,
beauty spreads from your eyes,
grace of God on you is pouring,
angels' songs lead you to paradise.

Preserve in you, O baby gentle,
the innocence of childhood days,
and God will lovingly direct you
to blissful happiness—always.

With thanks to Rudolph Knez and Edward Gobetz

NATIVE AMERICA/Abenaki

Cahwee dzidzis, dzidzis cahwee,
Tahwee dzidzis ohleegwahsi.

Sleep thou, baby, baby sleep thou,
In the tree, baby, have a good dream.

With thanks to Joseph Bruchac III

PUERTO RICO

Duerme, mi tesoro,
duerme, mi bien,
que los angelitos
te miran también.

Duérmete, ricura,
duérmete pronto,
que la negra noche lo obscurece todo.
Duérmete, ricura.

Sleep, my treasure,
sleep, my beloved,
let the little angels
watch over you as well.

Go to sleep, my sweet child,
go to sleep quickly,
let the dark night obscure all.
Go to sleep, my sweet child.

AFGHANISTAN

Aa lalo lalo lalo
Aa lalo bacha lalo

Baba ba shekaar raftah
Maadar bari kaar raftah

Aa lalo lalo lalo
Aa lalo bacha lalo

Aa lalo ai maapaarah
Maapaarah da gawaarah
Gawaarah tilaakaari
Bando baarish morwaari

Aa lalo lalo lalo
Aa lalo bacha lalo

Go to sleep, go to sleep,
Go to sleep, little child.

Your father is out hunting,
Your mother is busy working.

Go to sleep, go to sleep,
Go to sleep, little child.

Go to sleep, little moon,
Little moon in the cradle,
A cradle engraved with gold,
Decorated with pearls.

Go to sleep, go to sleep,
Go to sleep, little child.

آللو للو للو

آللو بچه للو

بابه به شکار رفته

مادر بر کار رفته

آللو للو للو

آللو بچه للو

آللو ای ماهپاره

ماهپاره ده گهواره

گهواره طلاکاری

بندو بارش مروار

آللو للو للو

آللو بچه للو

FINLAND

Tuutuuti pienoista.
Nuku armaani rauhassa.
Tähdet tuolla taivaalla
Kaikki lapsen lampaita.
Kuu on heillä paimenna,
Nuku armas rauhassa.

Uinu nyt tuutituu
Ruusuposki ja hymysuu.
Oi jos pienet jalkasi.
Aina teillä kulkisi,
Missä lapsen enkeli,
Ilomielin seuraisi.

Tuutuuti pienoista.
Nuku armaani rauhassa,
Kasva, kasva suureksi,
Aimo Suomen mieheksi.
Äiti kun käy vanhaksi
Lapsi varttuu turvaksi.

Tu, tu, tu, ti, little one.
Sleep in peace, precious little one.
High above the stars are lambs,
The shining moon their shepherd.
Off to sleep now, little one,
Sleep, my precious, dearest little one.

Now then sleep, tu, tu, tu, ti,
Rosy-cheeked and mouth so smiling,
May you always tread the good path.
May you follow the good angel,
So to sleep, sleep, little one,
Sleep, my precious, dearest little one.

Thrive and grow big, dearest one,
Grow to be a fine Finnish man.
Then when Mother will grow old
Her protector you will be.
Sleep, my baby, little one,
Sleep, my precious, dearest little one.

VENEZUELA

Duérmete, niño chiquito,
que tu madre no está aquí;
que se fue a buscar guayabas,
las mejores para ti.

Si este niño no se duerme,
¡qué noche pasaré yo!
Pasaré la noche en vela,
cantándole el arrorró.

Go to sleep, little child,
because your mother is not here;
she went to look for guavas,
the best ones for you.

If this child doesn't sleep,
what a night I'll have!
I'll spend the night in watch,
singing him a lullaby.

With thanks to Linda Mannheim

REPUBLIC OF KOREA

Chajang, chajang uri agi, chajang, chajang uri agi

Koko taka, uji mara. Uri agi chamul kkaella

Mong-mong kaeya, chitji mara. Uri agi chamul kkaella.

Chajang, chajang uri agi. Chajang, chajang uri agi.

Kumja-dong-ah, Unja-dong-ah. Uri agi chaldo jandah

Kumul joomyon noh-rul sa-myo, Unnul joomyon noh-rul sa-rya

Narah-eh-nun chungshin-dong-ah. Pumo-eh-nun hyoja-dong-ah

Chajang, chajang uri agi, chajang, chajang uri agi.

Sleep, sleep, our baby; sleep, sleep, our baby,

Do not crow, chicken, our baby might wake,

Do not bark, doggie, our baby might wake.

Sleep, sleep, our baby; sleep, sleep, our baby.

O golden baby, O silver baby, our baby sleeps well.

Could I buy you with gold? Could I buy you with silver?

Baby, loyal to your country, loyal to your parents,

Sleep, sleep, our baby; sleep, sleep, our baby.

With thanks to Yu Young-nan and Patricia McMahon

Mādare to torā dust dārad mesle jane khodash

Torā ruye cheshme khodash migozārad

Torā gorbān mishavad

IRAN

Lālā, lālā gole lale
Palang dar kuh che minale
Lālā, lālā gole khashkhāsh
Bābāt rafte khodā hamrāsh
Lālā, lālā gole abi
Cherā emshab nemikhābi
Lālā, lālā gole bādum
Bekhāb ārum, bekhāb ārum

Lullaby, lullaby, tulip flower,
The leopard is roaring on the mountain.
Lullaby, lullaby, poppy flower,
God keep your faraway father.
Lullaby, lullaby, water lily,
Why don't you go to sleep tonight?
Lullaby, lullaby, almond blossom,
Sleep in peace, sleep in peace.

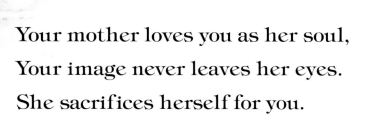

Your mother loves you as her soul,
Your image never leaves her eyes.
She sacrifices herself for you.

UGANDA (Luganda language)

Woowooto, woowooto,
Woowootera omwana yeebake.
Woowooto, woowooto,
Woowootera Babirye yeebake.

Woowooto, woowooto,
Siisiitira omwana yeebake.
Woowooto, woowooto,
Ffe twagala omwana kwebaka.

Woowooto, woowooto,
Omwana wa taata weebake.
Woowooto, woowooto,
Omwana wa maama omwagalwa.

Woowooto, woowooto,
Nkuyitire jjajja akwebase.
Woowooto, woowooto,
Omwoyo gwa maama gukuluma.

Woowooto, woowooto,
Akufumbira akamere weebake.
Woowooto, woowooto,
Zibiriza amaaso weebake.

Hush-a-bye, hush-a-bye,
Lull baby to sleep.
Hush-a-bye, hush-a-bye,
Lull Babirye to sleep.

Hush-a-bye, hush-a-bye,
Rock the baby to sleep.
Hush-a-bye, hush-a-bye,
We want our baby to go to sleep.

Hush-a-bye, hush-a-bye,
My daddy's baby, go to sleep.
Hush-a-bye, hush-a-bye,
My mama's baby she loves so much.

Hush-a-bye, hush-a-bye,
Shall I call Grandma to help you sleep?
Hush-a-bye, hush-a-bye,
Your heart aches for your mama.

Hush-a-bye, hush-a-bye,
She's cooking food for you, go to sleep.
Hush-a-bye, hush-a-bye,
Now close your eyes, sleep, baby, sleep.

CZECH REPUBLIC

Spi děťátko, spi.
Zavři očka svý.
Pán Bůh bude s tebou spáti,
Andělíčci kolébati,
Spi děťátko, spi.

Sleep, my baby, sleep.

Close your tiny eyes.

God will be with you as you sleep,

Guardian angels will rock you,

Sleep, my baby, sleep.

With thanks to Miriam Mareček

TURKEY

Ninni, yavrum, ninni,
Benim yavrumun uykusu var, ninni
Şimdi benim yavrum uyuyacak, ninni
E, e, e, e, e.

Ninni, yavrum, ninni,
Benim yavrumun uykusu var, ninni
Şimdi benim yavrum uyuyor, ninni
Benim yavrum uyuyup büyüyecek, ninni
E, e, e, e, e.

Ninni, yavrum, ninni,
Benim yavrum uyudu, ninni
Benim yavrum uyuyup büyüyecek, ninni
Tıpış tıpış yürüyecek, ninni
E, e, e, e, e.

Neennee, my darling neennee,
My darling is sleepy, neennee.
My darling now will sleep, neennee.
E, e, e, e, e.

Neennee, my darling neennee,
My darling is sleepy, neennee.
My darling now will sleep, neennee,
Will sleep and grow, neennee.
E, e, e, e, e.

Neennee, my darling neennee,
My darling is now asleep, neennee,
Will sleep and grow, neennee,
Soon will start to walk, neennee.
E, e, e, e, e.

With thanks to Nurcihan Kesim and Asli Karasuil

38

UNITED STATES

Hush, little baby, don't say a word,
Papa's gonna buy you a mockingbird.

And if that mockingbird don't sing,
Papa's gonna buy you a diamond ring.

And if that diamond ring turns brass,
Papa's gonna buy you a looking glass.

And if that looking glass gets broke,
Papa's gonna buy you a billy goat.

And if that billy goat won't pull,
Papa's gonna buy you a cart and bull.

And if that cart and bull turn over,
Papa's gonna buy you a dog named Rover.

And if that dog named Rover don't bark,
Papa's gonna buy you a horse and cart.

And if that horse and cart fall down,
You'll still be the prettiest little baby in town.

Jane Yolen is the author of more than one hundred books for children, young adults, and adults. Her *Owl Moon,* illustrated by John Schoenherr, won the 1988 Caldecott Medal. She has received the Kerlan Award for her body of work as well as the 1992 Regina Medal from the Catholic Library Association. Among her titles for Boyds Mills Press are *Jane Yolen's Mother Goose Songbook,* a 1993 International Reading Association/Children's Book Council Children's Choice, and *Street Rhymes Around the World.* She lives in Hatfield, Massachusetts.

Thailand: CHEWUN WISASA, a former art teacher, is a free-lance artist and a member of the Thai Section of the International Board on Books for Young People, ABC (Arts and Books for Children) Group. He was born in Bangkok and lives in Nakon Pathom.

Italy: MARIA BATTAGLIA, a former schoolteacher, is now a free-lance artist. She was born in Cuneo and lives in Bra.

Nigeria: CHARLES ONYEKWERE OHU is a free-lance artist who has illustrated books and magazines for children and adults. He was born in Bukuru, Plateau State, and makes his home in Mushim, Lagos State.

Wales: MARGARET D. JONES was born in Bromley, Kent, England, but has lived in Wales for almost forty years. She lives in Capel Bangor, Dyfed, where she works as a free-lance artist.

Ukraine: MARIA PECHENA is an artist who was born and lives in Kiev.

Slovenia: JANKO TESTEN is an artist and teacher who lives in Ljubljana, where he was born.

Native America/Abenaki: DAVID KANIETAKERON FADDEN, born in Lake Placid, New York, is a free-lance artist living in Onchiota, New York, where he manages the Six Nations Museum. His ancestors come from the Abenaki and Mohawk tribes.

Puerto Rico: JUAN ALVAREZ O'NEILL, born in San Juan, works as a free-lance artist for the newspaper *El Nuevo Dia* and for *Dialogo,* the newspaper of the University of Puerto Rico. He lives in Bayamón.

Afghanistan: MIRAJUDIN GHAWSI is an artist with the Instructional Material Development Center of the University of Nebraska at Omaha, which develops educational material for Afghanistan. Born in Kabul, he lives in exile in Peshawar, Pakistan.

Finland: KRISTIINA LOUHI, a native of Helsinki, illustrates children's books. She makes her home in Järvenpää.

Venezuela: MORELLA FUENMAYOR works as a free-lance artist in Caracas, where she was born.

Republic of Korea: KIM SEON MEE is a student at Duksung Women's University in Seoul, where she is studying fine art. She is a native of Seoul and currently resides there.

Iran: FEEROOZEH GOLMOHAMMADI is a photographer, magazine editor, writer, and illustrator of children's books. She was born in Tehran and still lives there.

Uganda: SIMON S.K. SAGALA-MULINDWA is a graphic designer for Makerere University and a free-lance artist. He is a native of Kampala, where he still resides.

Czech Republic: JAN ČERNÝ is a free-lance illustrator of children's books who was born in Prague and still resides there.

Turkey: MUSTAFA DELIOGLU worked in animation at an advertising agency and had his own studio before he created art for children's books. He was born in Erzincan and resides in Istanbul.

United States: CYD MOORE, a native of Shellman, Georgia, has illustrated a number of books for children. She lives in Birmingham, Michigan.

Jacket and Title Page: FRANÉ LESSAC, a free-lance artist, is from Jersey City, New Jersey. She lived in the Caribbean for many years and now resides in Fremantle, West Australia.